My Naughty Little Puppy

Rascal's Sleepover Fun

Slurp!

D0683026

For William ~ H.W.
For Si x ~ K.P.

Woof
magazine

STRIPES PUBLISHING
An imprint of Little Tiger Press
1 The Coda Centre,
189 Munster Road,
London SW6 6AW

A paperback original
First published in Great Britain
in 2011

Text copyright © Holly Webb, 2011
Illustrations copyright
© Kate Pankhurst, 2011, 2012

ISBN: 978-1-84715-157-5

The right of Holly Webb and Kate
Pankhurst to be identified as the
author and illustrator of this work
respectively has been asserted by
them in accordance with the
Copyright, Designs and Patents
Act, 1988.

A CIP catalogue record for this
book is available from the British
Library.

Printed and bound in China.

10 9 8 7 6 5 4 3 2

For more information
about Holly Webb visit:
www.holly-webb.com

My Naughty Little Puppy

HOLLY WEBB

Illustrated by
Kate Pankhurst

Stripes

Chapter One
Rascal Goes Shopping

"Wait there, Rascal. Good boy." Ellie patted Rascal's head, and he looked up at her, his bright eyes hopeful. There were yummy smells around here, and he was hungry. Rascal was always hungry, and the delicious whiff of bread wafting out of the supermarket door was actually making him dribble.

Ellie followed her mum, glancing over her shoulder at Rascal. "We won't be long," she called back to him, hoping he'd be all right. He wasn't used to being left alone, but Mum wanted to pop into the shop on the way back from their walk in the park.

"Perhaps I'd better stay with him," Ellie said anxiously.

Mum smiled. "He'll be fine, Ellie. We're only going to be quick. And I need you with me – they've got some lovely birthday cakes on show. I thought you could choose one, and then we can order it in plenty of time for your birthday."

Ellie nodded excitedly. "Back soon, Rascal!"

Rascal stared after Ellie, and gave a little whine. Where was Ellie going? He pulled at his lead, trying to follow her, but Ellie had tied it to a metal ring on the wall.

My Naughty Little Puppy

Ellie and her mum went into the shop,
and headed for the cakes at the far end.

"Ooh! Look at that one!" Ellie admired
the display of cakes, pointing out one with
a mermaid on the top, her tail trailing
around the side of the cake. "And there's a
gorgeous dog one –
but it's a Dalmatian.
Do you think they'd
make a Jack Russell
one, just like Rascal?"
Mum looked
doubtful. "I don't know,
I suppose we could ask."
"A chocolate cake –
with brown and white icing,"
Ellie added hopefully.

But Mum was frowning. "What on earth's going on over there?"

Two shop assistants, followed by a security guard calling into his radio, went running past the end of the aisle. Ellie turned round and tried to see where they were going.

"No, apparently he's not very fierce – but you never know..." the guard was saying into his radio.

Ellie looked up at Mum, her eyes wide with horror. She had a dreadful feeling that she knew who "he" was.

"You tied Rascal up, didn't you, Ellie?" Mum asked.

"Yes, of course!" Ellie said quickly. "But you know what Rascal's like..." she added.

My Naughty Little Puppy

Mum nodded grimly. She certainly did. Ellie and her family had only had Rascal for three months, but he'd managed to get into an awful lot of trouble in such a short time.

Ellie still half-hoped that all the fuss was nothing to do with them, and that her puppy was sitting outside, as good as gold. But then a sharp bark echoed round the shop, and Rascal raced joyfully up the aisle to her, his lead trailing along behind him, and the remains of a packet of expensive-looking biscuits in his mouth.

Rascal dropped the biscuits and leaped into Ellie's arms, licking her delightedly all over her face. He hadn't known where she was, and he was very glad to see her.

"Let's get him out of here, Ellie," Mum

muttered, picking up what was left of the pack of biscuits. Just then, the security guard caught up with them.

"I take it he's yours then?" he asked, frowning at Rascal.

"I'm very sorry!" Ellie gasped. "I left him tied up outside, I really did! He must have managed to pull his lead undone somehow, and then he came looking for me."

"We just popped in for a moment," Mum murmured. "We'll take him home ... and of course I'll pay for the biscuits..."

"Don't let it happen again!" the security guard told them sternly, and as Ellie and Mum hurried off, he added, "And buy a book on knots!"

"Honestly, Ellie! I've never been so embarrassed." Mum's face was scarlet as she quickly paid for the biscuits. "I don't think I'll ever be able to come here again!"

Rascal leaned over Ellie's shoulder, looking wistfully back into the place with all the good smells. He was glad he'd found Ellie, but why did they have to leave so soon?

Ellie and Mum walked home rather fast, with Rascal scampering beside them. Mum was still pink-cheeked with embarrassment, and Ellie was wondering if this meant she wouldn't be getting her birthday cake after all. But Mum would get over it – wouldn't she?

Now probably wasn't the moment to ask about her party again, though. She was really hoping to have a sleepover, but Mum didn't seem all that keen on the idea. When Ellie had first asked Mum had said she'd think about it, and she still hadn't said yes or no. Mum wasn't sure if there was space in Ellie's tiny room for anyone except Ellie, although Ellie reckoned they could just about fit in her best friend Christy and her other friends Jessie and Lydia – although they might not be able to breathe, all squashed together on Ellie's bedroom floor.

"I really did tie him up, Mum," she said quietly.

Her mum looked down at her and sighed. "I know, Ellie. It wasn't really your fault. I shouldn't have suggested leaving him on his own outside a shop. He's still only little – he didn't understand what was going on."

Ellie looked down at Rascal. He glanced back up at her, his eyes sparkling, and she couldn't help but smile. Sometimes

My Naughty Little Puppy

she suspected that Rascal actually liked being naughty – but she loved him anyway.

Chapter Two

Someone New

"It felt like everyone in the shop was staring at us!" Ellie told Christy, kicking her heels against the wall where they were sitting in the playground before school. "It was so embarrassing. I've been keeping Rascal out of Mum's way ever since."

Christy sighed. "I don't suppose you've asked about your party then?"

Ellie shook her head. "And it's only two weeks away now, no one will be

able to come if I don't hurry up."

"Ooh, I forgot to tell you, I had an idea!" Christy bounced up from the wall. "You know your mum's worried about fitting us all in? Well, why don't we sleep in the living room instead? There's lots of space on the floor in there."

Ellie nodded slowly. "And then I could use my sleeping bag too!" she agreed. It had sounded a bit boring being in her normal bed when everyone else was snuggled up in sleeping bags. "That's a fab idea. I'll ask Mum after school."

"That's what I did with my cousins when I went to stay with them, it was really fun." Christy giggled. "I didn't go to sleep until midnight, though."

My Naughty Little Puppy

Ellie wrinkled her nose. "I don't think my mum would let us get away with that."

Christy grinned. "You never know. If she's upstairs, she might not be able to hear us."

Everyone was chatting before registration when Mr Turner came in with a strange girl in a Chase Hill uniform.

"Must be the new girl!" Christy whispered. "I forgot she was starting today." Mrs Harley had told them the week before that someone new was joining their class, and they had to make a special effort to look after her as it was hard to move schools near the end of the year.

My Naughty Little Puppy

"She looks nice. She's got pretty hair,"
Ellie murmured back. The new girl had very
long curly dark hair in two bunches, with
pink ballet shoes on her hairbands. She
also looked very shy – she was almost
hiding behind the headmaster.

My Naughty Little Puppy

Mrs Harley stood up and introduced her. "Everyone, this is Lucy, who's joining our class. I'm sure you'll all do your best to make her feel welcome. Who'd like to help look after her?" She looked round the class, as lots of the girls waved their hands excitedly. Ellie put up her hand too – it would be fun to show someone new around. "Ellie, yes, perfect. Make sure you take good care of her, won't you? Come and ask me if there's anything you need help with. Lucy, this is Ellie, and her friend Christy. They'll tell you everything you need to know."

Ellie and Christy nodded, and Lucy came to sit next to Ellie. Her face was bright pink, as though she hated everyone looking at her.

My Naughty Little Puppy

At break, Ellie and Christy took Lucy outside with them. "Have you just moved here?" Ellie asked.

Lucy nodded. "Last week." Her voice was hardly more than a whisper.

"Do you like ballet?" Ellie asked, trying hard to think of something to say.

Lucy smiled. "Yes, I love it. I really want to find a dance class to go to here."

"There's a ballet class at the village hall," Ellie said thoughtfully. "I go there to take my puppy to training, and I'm sure I've seen a poster."

"Christy! Do you want to play Chain-It?" someone called from across the playground.

"Coming," Christy yelled back. "Do you want to play, Lucy?" she added politely.

My Naughty Little Puppy

Lucy looked doubtful. "I'm not very good at running..."

"Me neither." Ellie laughed. "Christy's super-fast, she loves running. She beat all the boys at Sports Day a couple of weeks ago. We'll watch."

Christy shrugged, and ran off to join the game.

My Naughty Little Puppy

"Thanks," Lucy said. "I always get stuck being 'It' for ages, I hate that."

"Me too," Ellie agreed. "I'm just not very sporty."

"Do you like dancing?" Lucy asked hopefully.

"I like dancing at parties and things, but I've never done lessons." Ellie looked thoughtful, remembering her birthday. She wondered if Lucy would like to come to her sleepover – if she was allowed one. She'd only known Lucy for a morning, but the new girl seemed really nice. And she was supposed to be making her feel welcome.

My Naughty Little Puppy

Ellie checked the poster in the village hall that night when Dad took her and Rascal to dog-training. She carefully wrote down the phone number.

"Are *you* going to do ballet?" someone said scornfully behind her.

Ellie tensed up, recognizing the voice. Amelia was in Year Six at her school, and she was horrible.

"I don't think that's a good idea, Ellie," Amelia went on. "Not going by how often you fall over in dog-training."

Ellie opened and shut her mouth, desperately trying to think of something to say back, but Amelia just snorted and went on into the hall, with Goldie, her pretty spaniel, trotting behind her.

My Naughty Little Puppy

"Do you think we could ask Jo if she does another class we can go to, just to get away from her?" Ellie's friend Jack had come in behind Amelia. His huge Great Dane Hugo stood there patiently while Rascal jumped up and yapped as if to say "hello".

Ellie sighed. "Goldie's so perfect, I'm just hoping Amelia's mum decides she doesn't need any more training." She giggled. "Somehow I don't think that's ever going to happen with Rascal!" She told

My Naughty Little Puppy

Jack about the supermarket incident as they went into the hall, where Jo, their instructor, was welcoming everyone.

"We're going to start training the puppies off the lead tonight," she explained. "It's really important that when you let your dog loose they come back when they're called, whatever else is going on around them. It's a tricky thing to learn, and I have to say, some dogs are just never going to be safe off the lead."

Amelia smirked. "Goldie always comes when I call. I let her off the lead in the park all the time."

Ellie and Jack rolled their eyes at each other. But Ellie couldn't help wondering whether Rascal would ever learn.

Chapter Three

Party Plans

Ellie went home from dog-training feeling that she and Rascal still needed lots more practice.

"Did you have a good time?" Mum asked.

Ellie nodded. "Rascal didn't do anything too bad," she promised. "We're doing training off the lead. He was OK while I was close, but he got distracted really easily. I'm going to practise with him at

the weekend. Oh, and I got this phone number for Lucy, the new girl I told you about. She's looking for a ballet class."

Mum smiled. "That's nice. Maybe she'd like to come to your party."

Ellie looked up at her hopefully. "Does that mean I can have a sleepover?" She'd told Mum Christy's idea when she got home from school.

"Yes. But only four friends."

"Thanks, Mum!" Ellie picked up Rascal and hugged him. "It's going to be brilliant! I can't wait to tell Christy! You can sleep on my sleeping bag, Rascal!"

But Christy was late to school the next morning. Ellie strode up and down the playground fence, desperate to tell her

My Naughty Little Puppy

best friend the exciting news.

"Hi, Ellie," someone said shyly behind her, as she checked her watch for what seemed like the hundredth time.

Ellie turned round. "Hi, Lucy."

"Are you OK?"

"I was just waiting for Christy. I wanted to tell her, my mum's said I can have a sleepover for my birthday." She smiled a little shyly at Lucy. "Would you like to come?"

"Really?" Lucy's face lit up with excitement. "I'd love to. Um, when is it?"

"Two weeks' time. Not this Saturday but the next one. Oh, there's Christy!" Ellie grabbed Lucy's hand and towed her towards the gate. "Christy! Christy! Mum said yes! Can you come? Lucy's coming too!"

My Naughty Little Puppy

Ellie was so excited about her
sleepover that she didn't notice that Christy
wasn't quite as pleased as she ought to
have been.

"Oh, cool," she murmured, and as the
bell rang she followed Ellie and Lucy into
school with a surprised, slightly hurt look
on her face.

My Naughty Little Puppy

"FOUR? Four extra girls?" Max stared at Mum with his mouth open in horror. "All night?"

Mum nodded, and then thought for a moment. "Would you like me to arrange with Lewis's mum for you to stay the night?"

Max nodded eagerly. "Yes, please!"

"Can I go too?" Dad murmured, grinning at Ellie, and she pretended to elbow him in the side.

"Why don't I ever get to have four mates to sleep over?" Max asked, scowling down at his dinner plate.

Mum rolled her eyes. "Because I like my house the way it is, thank you. I've seen what you can do, five of you would be like a wrecking ball."

Lila shuddered. "I don't even want to think about it. Ellie, do you want me to help you decorate the house for your party?"

Ellie gazed at her delightedly. "Please!" She could feel Rascal wagging his tail against her leg under the table. She was sure he was as excited about the party as she was.

After tea, Ellie raced upstairs. She'd finished her homework when she got back from school, and now she got out her best paper and pens, and the pots of glitter that Auntie Gemma had given her at Christmas. Carefully, she began to design her party invitations, dabbing the glue on to make a

glittery paw-print shape. Rascal sat on her
lap, trying to lick the glue. Then he sniffed
eagerly at the glitter, but it made him sneeze.

"Oh, Rascal!" Ellie was half-laughing,
half-cross. "Look, it's everywhere!" She tilted
her head to one side, eyeing the purple
and silver swirly pattern that Rascal had
managed to create. "Actually, that's quite
nice, Rascal..."

Chapter Four
A Milky Mess

The next morning, when the glitter had had time to dry, Ellie proudly tucked her invitations into envelopes that she'd decorated. She was really looking forward to giving them out to her friends. She carried the invitations downstairs and put them next to her on the kitchen table, so she wouldn't forget them.

"You did remember to put the time on, didn't you?" Mum asked.

My Naughty Little Puppy

"And 'RSVP'." Ellie nodded, pouring herself some cereal, while Mum yelled up the stairs to Max and Lila to hurry. Rascal pattered over from his breakfast bowl – which he had left sparkling clean – and looked up at her hopefully. Sometimes Ellie dropped him a cornflake or two.

Ellie was dreamily eating her cornflakes, and she didn't notice Rascal sneakily jumping on to the chair next to hers, and then lunging across the table for the little pile of cornflakes she'd accidentally spilled out of the box.

Suddenly, his back paws slipped on the chair. He scrabbled desperately at the table and sent the carton of milk flying. All over one of the invitations.

"Oh, no! Rascal, look what you've done!" Ellie wailed.

Rascal wriggled back on to the chair and looked up at her guiltily, his ears flattened against his head. He stuck his

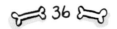

nose between his paws and whined sadly. He knew that he'd done something wrong.

Mum ran back in. "What happened?"

"My invitation!" Ellie snatched it up, and quickly moved the others out of the way of the spreading tide of milk, while Mum grabbed a dishcloth.

Mum looked closer and sighed. "Oh, dear. Which one was it?"

That was just the right word, Ellie realized sadly. It was an invitation, and now it wasn't. It hung from her fingers like a limp rag. She peeled the envelope open, and read the blurry words. "It's Christy's. Oh, and I made it extra beautiful! What am I going to do?"

Mum frowned. "I really think you need

to give them out today, time's a bit tight, otherwise I'd say make her a new one this evening."

"I can do you one on the computer if you like," Lila suggested from the doorway, where she'd seen what was going on.

"Thanks, Lila!" Ellie hugged her.

Rascal whined again, from under the chair now, looking up at Ellie with his big brown eyes. He'd jumped down as soon as Mum came back in.

"Oh, Rascal." Ellie crouched down to stroke him. "You're a little menace, you really are." She could never be cross with Rascal for long.

My Naughty Little Puppy

Ellie handed out the invitations as soon as she got to school. She really hoped Christy wouldn't mind that hers was different. Lila had done her best, but it just wasn't as special as the glittery ones Ellie had worked so hard on.

It was a pity that Christy had to see Lucy's one, Ellie realized, as she watched her two friends excitedly tearing open their envelopes. Maybe she should have explained what had happened first.

My Naughty Little Puppy

Lucy beamed as she opened the
envelope. "It's so pretty! Did you make it?"
Ellie nodded.

Christy's cheeks went pink as she looked
over at Lucy's invite. She quickly stuffed her
own plain one into her bag. "I can come,"

she muttered. "I already asked Mum."

"That's great!" Ellie tried to hug her, but Christy backed away.

"I'm just going to talk to Jessie and Lydia," she said, then ran off across the playground.

Ellie stared after her, hardly hearing Lucy's excited questions about the party.

Christy seemed really quiet all day. She didn't hang around with Ellie and Lucy at all at break or lunch, just went straight off to play some energetic game with the others.

Ellie was worried Christy was upset about the invitation, but she didn't want to abandon Lucy to go and ask. Maybe she was just imagining it? At least she and Christy were walking home together tonight, they could talk on their own then. But the day seemed to drag on forever.

Chapter Five

Best Friends Forever?

After school, Ellie walked out with Lucy, who was chattering about her mum signing her up for the new ballet class. Christy trailed behind them.

Mum waved to them from the gate, and Rascal barked excitedly, jumping around on the end of his lead.

Ellie smiled. She couldn't be miserable when she got a welcome like that. She hurried forward, and crouched down to

hug him. Rascal licked her all over, and Ellie laughed, looking back to introduce him to Lucy.

"Lucy, this is my dog, Rascal!" Ellie took his lead from Mum – or tried to. It slipped through her fingers as Rascal saw Christy behind Lucy, and leaped up excitedly to say "hello", with loud and joyful woofs.

My Naughty Little Puppy

Lucy screamed, and Ellie almost did too, she was so surprised. Rascal wasn't being fierce, he just wanted to be friendly. Frightened, he slunk back to Ellie, and she grabbed a tight hold on his lead.

"He won't hurt you," she told Lucy. "He just saw Christy and wanted to say 'hello'..." She trailed off. Lucy was so pale.

"I'd better go," Lucy whispered. "There's my mum. Bye, Ellie. Bye, Christy."

Ellie looked at Christy in horror, but her best friend just shrugged.

Mum stared after Lucy worriedly. "Oh dear, was that your new friend? She's not used to dogs, is she?"

Ellie sighed and nodded. "Come on, Rascal," she murmured, pulling Christy with her. As soon as they'd got far enough ahead of Mum, she asked, "Are you upset with me? It was an accident about the invitation, I promise it was! I'd made you a really nice one, and Rascal spilled milk all over it."

Christy nodded, but she didn't look very convinced.

"You didn't even talk to me today," Ellie went on, hating the way her voice sounded whingey.

"You haven't talked to *me* since Lucy came," Christy muttered.

"I promised Mrs Harley I'd look after her!" Ellie cried.

"That doesn't mean inviting her to your party!" Christy burst out.

My Naughty Little Puppy

Ellie stared at her, hurt. "But I like her..."

Christy glared back. "More than me?"

"No!" Ellie shook her head, and Rascal looked up, glancing between them anxiously. "Of course not!"

My Naughty Little Puppy

"Well, that's what it looks like!" Christy snapped, and marched off down the road, slamming her garden gate behind her.

Ellie stared after her. Today was supposed to have been so special, and it was ruined – Christy was furious with her, and Lucy was scared of Rascal. How on earth was she supposed to have a fun birthday sleepover now?

As soon as she'd got home, Ellie had raced up to her bedroom and burst into tears. A few minutes later, Lila put her head round the door. "Mum said you'd had a row with Christy. Want to talk about it?"

Ellie sniffed, and told her what had

My Naughty Little Puppy

happened with the invites.

"Don't worry, Ellie. You've been friends with Christy since Reception," Lila pointed out, sitting on the bed next to Ellie and hugging her. "She'll get over it."

"But my party!" Ellie wailed.

My Naughty Little Puppy

Lila frowned. "Perhaps you need to do something nice, just the two of you. Christy's feeling left out because you want to be friends with Lucy, too."

"Maybe I have been hanging around with Lucy a lot..." Ellie blew her nose. "But Christy's still my best friend."

"Prove it to her then."

Ellie thought. "I could invite her to the park with me and Rascal at the weekend."

"There you go. But try and find a time to ask her when it's just you," Lila suggested.

Ellie nodded. It would be tricky, but hopefully she could talk to Christy properly after school. Lucy was going to her first ballet class tomorrow.

My Naughty Little Puppy

It was torture sitting through a whole day next to a silent, miserable Christy. After school, Ellie waited behind her in the cloakroom, and put a hand on her arm.

Christy jumped. "You scared me!"

"Sorry. Christy, listen, I didn't mean to upset you by being friends with Lucy."

"It just seems like you're with her all the time..." Christy muttered, as they walked out to the gate.

"Only because I offered to make her feel welcome. She's nice, but you're my best friend!" Ellie laughed. "And Rascal's - look!"

Rascal barked delightedly as he saw them.

My Naughty Little Puppy

"Do you want to come to the park with me and Rascal on Saturday? And Bouncer too?" Ellie asked hopefully, as Rascal threw himself at her and Christy, whining and scrabbling at their knees.

"Yes. Yes, definitely!" Christy laughed and hugged Rascal, and smiled gratefully at Ellie, and then hugged her too.

My Naughty Little Puppy

"You don't mind about me asking Lucy to the party?" Ellie asked anxiously.

Christy shook her head. "No, I was just being stupid. She's nice."

But Ellie watched Rascal worriedly as he jumped around. She was friends with Christy again, and that was fab, but what was she going to do about Lucy? How could Lucy come to her sleepover party if she was terrified of Rascal?

Chapter Six

Rascal on the Loose

Ellie had been practising letting Rascal off the lead and calling him back in the garden, and she was feeling pretty hopeful about their trip to the park with Christy and Bouncer on Saturday. Jo had suggested that everyone practised calling their dogs lots – even indoors – and then making a big fuss and giving them a treat when they came. Ellie was sure that Rascal understood what "Come!" meant, and she'd been

My Naughty Little Puppy

using his favourite squeaky bone
to encourage him to come, too.

The park close to her house was one
where dogs were allowed to be off-lead as
long as they were under control. Ellie was
really looking forward to letting Rascal run
around with Bouncer without worrying
about him getting all tangled up in his lead.

"Jo said we had to make sure our
puppies come even if they are distracted,
so I got Max to throw a ball around at the
other end of the garden. He still came back
to me!" Ellie told Christy proudly. "The only
thing is we haven't been able to practise
with other dogs around. I think if there are
lots I might not let him off – just in case."

Christy nodded. "You can never tell with

some dogs, whether they're going to be friendly or not. And some owners aren't even looking!"

They'd deliberately come to the park early in the morning, so it was quite empty, and after a good run around to wear off some of Rascal's energy, Ellie unclipped his lead. She was trying to feel confident – she knew that if she sounded worried when she called Rascal, he'd pick up on it and be naughty. Rascal looked up at her curiously, as though he wasn't really sure he was allowed to go.

Ellie smiled. "Off you go! Chase Bouncer!" She let Rascal run about with Bouncer for a bit, and then decided she'd call him back just to make sure he came –

then she could make a fuss of him. Jo had explained how important it was to make the recall fun. Ellie watched carefully, picking a moment when Rascal was running in her direction anyway, to make it easier for him to do as he was told.

"Rascal! Rascal! Come!" she called loudly, trying to sound as though she was certain he'd obey her.

My Naughty Little Puppy

Rascal raced towards her eagerly, and
Ellie laughed in delight. "Good boy,
Rascal! Yay!" She patted him lovingly, and
gave him one of the little bone-shaped
biscuits he loved.

"He's got so much better," Christy said
admiringly.

Ellie beamed at her. "He's a star."

She'd brought Max's Frisbee, which
Rascal loved to chase in the garden. Here in

the park they'd be able to throw it much further, without worrying about it going over the fence. Rascal was so excited when he saw her pull it out of her rucksack that he barked non-stop.

Ellie laughed. "OK, ready?" She hurled the yellow Frisbee across the park, and Rascal set off after it like a little brown and white bullet, then launched himself into a huge leap to catch it out of the air.

My Naughty Little Puppy

"Wow, he is good," Christy said, as Rascal galloped back across the park, stopping every so often to give the Frisbee a really good shake. He brought it back to Ellie, and stood there with his tail wagging hopefully.

Ellie took it back – avoiding the slobbery side – and threw it for him again. The Frisbee curled out across the park, and Rascal raced away. It was only then that Ellie noticed the cyclist riding along the path. It was a boy about their age. He was riding really fast, and Ellie realized with horror that Rascal was going to cut straight across his path. Rascal only had eyes for the Frisbee, and the cyclist wasn't looking for small dogs coming at him sideways.

My Naughty Little Puppy

"Rascal! Rascal! COME!" Ellie shouted, but she knew she hadn't a chance – Rascal was concentrating on the Frisbee, and he went on running straight for the bike.

The boy on the bike saw Rascal at the very last minute, and pulled up with a screech of brakes, the bike twisting round and falling over sideways – with him underneath.

Ellie gave a horrified gasp, and she and Christy ran to help.

As the boy struggled out from under his bike, he murmured, "Hi, Ellie. Hey, Christy."

"Josh! Are you OK?" Ellie gazed down at him in surprise – it was one of the boys from their class. She helped Christy pick up his bike. "You're not hurt, are you? I'm so

sorry – Rascal was chasing his Frisbee,
I don't think he even saw you."

"I'm fine," said Josh, as he slowly got
to his feet.

Meanwhile, Rascal had come trotting
back, the Frisbee dangling from his mouth.
He spat it out at Ellie's feet. She picked him
up, her heart thumping. It looked like he
and Josh had had a narrow escape.

"I thought I was going to hit him," Josh admitted. "That's why I pulled up so fast."

"It's OK, it was my fault," Ellie told him shakily, clipping on Rascal's lead again. "I'm just really glad you're not hurt. See you on Monday, anyway."

Josh pedalled off, looking a bit wobbly, and Ellie and Christy exchanged glances.

"I think that's enough practice for now," said Christy. "Let's go home!"

Chapter Seven

Party Planners

At dog-training on Monday evening Jo was really impressed with Ellie and Rascal's recall, and stopped her after the class to make a fuss of Rascal.

"But we tried it in the park, and he nearly got run over by a bike," Ellie admitted. She explained about the Frisbee, and Jo nodded. "That just sounds to me like bad luck. Rascal's done really well, but there was no way he was going to come

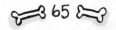

My Naughty Little Puppy

back in the middle of fetching his toy. You need to keep practising, that's all."

Rascal wagged his tail, as though he thought Jo was right.

"I was going to ask you, is there any way I can stop Rascal jumping up at people?" Ellie asked hopefully. "I'm having some friends round for my birthday, and one of them, Lucy, is nervous around dogs.

Rascal jumped up before and she got really upset." Ellie sighed. "He was only being friendly. I don't see how anyone could be scared of him!"

My Naughty Little Puppy

"Your friend probably can't help it,"
Jo said. "The tricky thing is that dogs can
sense when people are nervous, and
sometimes it makes them worse!" She
looked down at Rascal thoughtfully. "This is
going to sound weird, but the best thing to
do is ignore him when he jumps up at you.
If you give him any attention, it's only going
to make him more excited. Turn your back
on him and walk away. And if he sees you
and doesn't jump up, reward him for it, but
you've got to be calm, or he might get
excited and jump up again. I'm sorry, Ellie,
it's not something you can cure overnight.
Could you shut him in a different room
while your friend is round?"

Ellie sighed, and nodded. She supposed

it was the obvious answer, but she'd really
wanted Rascal to be part of her birthday.

That week at school Ellie and her friends
spent every spare moment planning the
sleepover.

"Are we going to watch a DVD?" Lydia
asked at break on Wednesday, and Ellie
blinked worriedly. She hadn't actually
thought about what they were going to do.
"I'm still thinking," she said quickly.

Ellie went back into class frowning.
A DVD... That was what everybody did.

"What's the matter?" Christy hissed,
while Mrs Harley was fiddling with the
interactive whiteboard.

My Naughty Little Puppy

"I want to think of something really fun to do at the party," Ellie whispered back, glancing between Christy and Lucy.

Christy frowned thoughtfully. "Would Max let us use his PlayStation?"

My Naughty Little Puppy

Ellie shrugged. "It isn't really his, it belongs to all of us, it's just usually Max who plays on it. But would it be that fun?"

Lucy poked Ellie's arm excitedly. "I've got this great dance game! Where you all have to dance along with the people on the screen, and you sing as well!"

"I love karaoke!" Christy whispered. "And you can teach us the dancing, Lucy!"

Ellie beamed – she felt like dancing round the classroom right then, only she couldn't because they were supposed to be in the middle of literacy. Lucy and Christy were getting on together, and her party was actually starting to sound like fun!

My Naughty Little Puppy

Max had (very grumpily) agreed that Ellie
and the others could use the PlayStation,
but there were lots of other things on Ellie's
perfect party list.

Number one was getting Rascal to
behave around Lucy. Ellie had grabbed the
chance to talk to her at lunch on Thursday,
when Christy was at tennis club. She didn't
want to embarrass Lucy.

"Are you going to be OK at my house?
With Rascal there, I mean?" Ellie asked
carefully.

Lucy looked down at her feet. "I'll try.
I just get scared when dogs jump up."

Ellie nodded. She'd been practising Jo's
special method, but it wasn't going very well.
When she walked away from Rascal he ran

round her in circles. Last night she'd ended
up tripping over him twice.

"He's very friendly," she told Lucy.

Her friend nodded sadly. "I know. He's
really sweet. I just can't help it."

"Don't worry," said Ellie. "I can shut him
in the kitchen."

Lucy gave her a grateful look, and Ellie
smiled at her, but inside she couldn't help
wishing there was another way.

Chapter Eight

The Big Day

"Happy birthday, Ellie!" Grandad was almost hidden behind an enormous present.

"Thanks, Grandad." Ellie beamed, taking the parcel. She had no idea what it could be. Her birthday present list, which she'd given to Grandad, Grandma and Auntie Gemma, as well as Mum and Dad, had been quite short. All she could think of were new dog books, fun craft stuff and toys for Rascal. Mum and Dad had surprised her with a fantastic camera, the first one she'd ever had of her own. It already had about thirty pictures of Rascal on it. But so far her favourite present was Auntie Gemma's – a set of dog bowls to paint herself. She was really looking forward to decorating them with Rascal's name.

"Anyone would think you liked dogs, Ellie." Max had smirked, as she opened her presents.

"What is it?" said Ellie. The parcel felt squishy and was strangely light.

Grandad laughed. "Open it and see!"

Ellie sat down at the kitchen table, which was already covered in wrapping paper and bits of ribbon, as well as a pile of opened presents. It was so nice that her birthday was

My Naughty Little Puppy

on a Saturday this year, and she didn't have
to rush off to school. And Mum was making
pancakes for breakfast – her favourite.

Rascal was enjoying Ellie's birthday, too.
Standing with his paws on a chair, he nibbled
the wrapping paper. He loved the way it
crinkled. He then sniffed the pile of presents,
and tugged at the ear of a big pink fluffy
rabbit. It smelled good, and it looked chewy.

My Naughty Little Puppy

"Oh, that's lovely." Mum laughed as Ellie showed her Grandad's present – a blue cushion with a photo of Rascal's face on it. "Did you get it printed?"

"Yes, at that T-shirt place. Do you like it?"

Ellie nodded, as Lila came over to have a look. "It's such a nice photo of Rascal!"

"I thought you could put it on the window seat in your room." Grandad beamed. "Anyway, I'll leave you to have breakfast," he said, getting to his feet. "All ready for the party then?"

Max groaned, and Mum frowned at him. "Don't, Max. Just be grateful you hadn't already gone to stay at Lewis's, or you might have caught his bug, and you'd be throwing up too."

My Naughty Little Puppy

"I *will* be throwing up," Max muttered.
"House full of girls dancing. Using my
PlayStation!"

Ellie and Lila rolled their eyes at each
other.

My Naughty Little Puppy

"Everything's ready," Mum assured Grandad. "The cake's hidden away – Ellie chose a lovely chocolate layer cake – and we've got loads of party food. We just need to put up the decorations. But, Ellie, you need to ring Gran and Grandpa first. They'll want to hear that you got their present."

Ellie nodded. They had sent her the pink fluffy rabbit. To be honest, Ellie thought it was a bit babyish, but it was very cute.

"Where is it?" she asked Mum, looking at the pile of presents.

Mum lifted up some of the wrapping paper, looking confused. "It must be here somewhere!" Then she frowned. "Rascal..."

Ellie looked under the table. No Rascal,

which was odd, because he was usually wherever she was.

Then Rascal trotted back into the kitchen looking innocent. *Who, me?* his dark eyes seemed to say. Ellie darted out into the hallway, but there was no telltale trail of pink fluff.

"Has he hidden it somewhere?" Dad asked. "He was playing with it before. Maybe he just took a fancy to it, for some odd reason... Not that I mean it's not nice," he added hurriedly. Ellie giggled.

Mum sighed. "Just call Gran and Grandpa and tell them you like it. I'm sure it'll turn up."

My Naughty Little Puppy

"More balloons on the banisters?" Lila
asked thoughtfully. They had put up loads
of streamers before lunch, and now it was
just the balloons left for a finishing touch.

Ellie stood back to admire the effect.
"No. I think we should put the rest in the
living room." She'd been having trouble
with the balloons before Lila came to help
– Rascal kept trying to eat the dangling
ribbons. But now he seemed to have lost
interest and had wandered off.

Ellie gave Lila an excited hug. "Thanks
for helping."

Lila grinned. "Makes up for Max..."

"Oi! I heard that," Max growled, as he
walked past. He was still grumpy about
Lewis being ill.

My Naughty Little Puppy

Ellie frowned. She hoped Max wasn't going to be too much of a pain tonight. She looked at the clock. Only about ten minutes before everyone arrived!

A sudden shriek from the kitchen made her jump.

"You bad dog!"

Rascal shot out into the hallway, looking guilty. He seemed different...

It took Ellie a moment to realize that he hadn't grown brown-coloured patches all over his face since she'd last seen him.

He'd been eating her chocolate birthday cake.

Chapter Nine

Birthday Disaster!

"The cake!" Mum groaned. "He's eaten the whole of one corner. I don't think there's any way of saving it, I'm sorry, Ellie."

Ellie sat down on the stairs. How could she have a party with no birthday cake? Everyone would be here in a minute, too. She knew it wouldn't really help, and she didn't want to make Mum feel even worse, but she could feel her eyes filling with tears.

"I didn't know he'd got into the kitchen..."

she whispered sadly, as Mum came and sat down next to her.

"It's not your fault, Ellie. I got it out and put it on the table, and then your Auntie Gemma phoned to say happy birthday to you... I should have been more careful."

Dad was eyeing Rascal worriedly. "How much of it did he eat? Chocolate isn't good for dogs. Do we need to take him to the vet?"

Ellie gasped in horror. She remembered reading in one of her dog books that dogs could get really ill from eating chocolate. She looked over at Rascal, who was licking thoughtfully at his chocolatey moustache.

"Don't panic." Mum hugged her. "It's only chocolate cake, not pure chocolate.

My Naughty Little Puppy

He might end up with a bit of a funny tummy, but I'm sure that's all. We'll just have to keep a close eye on him. But right now, I'm more worried about the cake than Rascal. What are we going to do?"

My Naughty Little Puppy

"What about birthday cupcakes?" Lila suggested. "Emily's big sister got married last weekend, she was a bridesmaid and she was showing the photos off at school. They had cupcakes instead of a big wedding cake, and they looked fab. Me and Dad could go and get all the ingredients. The supermarket has lovely icing flowers and things."

"What do you think, Ellie? You girls could all make them together." Mum stroked her cheek, and Ellie nodded. "That would be nice," she murmured. It would be fun to have a do-it-yourself birthday cake.

"We'll get lots of Smarties to go on top too," Dad promised. "So you'll still have your chocolatey cake."

"But we'll be keeping them away from Rascal," Mum added grimly.

"Someone's here!" Lila said, as the doorbell rang. "Come on, Dad! Emergency cake mission!"

"I'm not ready yet!" Ellie wailed. "Who is it?"

"It's me!" Christy poked her head round the front door as Lila opened it. "Sorry, am I early? Happy birthday!" From behind her back she whipped out a beautiful present in spotty paper and gave it to Ellie. "Er ... is that what you're wearing?" she asked, eyeing Ellie's grubby old jeans.

Ellie sniffed. "No. I've got a dress for the party, but I didn't have time to change. Oh, Christy, Rascal's eaten my cake!"

My Naughty Little Puppy

"He didn't!" Christy gasped in horror.

"We're going to make cupcakes instead, but I still think my party's going to be a disaster," Ellie said sadly.

Christy shook her head. "No, it won't. I love cupcakes. Look, I'll put Rascal in the garden to keep him away from Lucy. You go and get changed, quick!"

My Naughty Little Puppy

"They smell so good!" Christy closed her eyes blissfully. "Can we ice them yet?"

Ellie held her hand over the wire rack of cupcakes and shook her head. "Nope. Still too hot. The icing would just run off again. Be patient." She giggled – she sounded like her mum.

The girls were gathered in the kitchen, admiring the decorations that Lila and Dad had bought. There was even a pretty cardboard stand to put the cupcakes on when they were finished, so they'd look really professional.

"You could make up the icing, though," Mum suggested. "By the time you've done that, they might have cooled down."

"I'm going to cover mine in pink and green Smarties," Lydia decided, as she took her turn stirring the bowl of icing. "This is such a cool idea, Ellie. I'm going to have cupcakes at my birthday too."

Ellie felt Lila nudge her foot under the table. Her big sister grinned as she

dolloped the icing into small bowls, so they could make up lots of different colours, and Mum handed out the cakes.

"Can I do one?" Max asked, and Ellie glared at him suspiciously. But she could hardly say no. She passed along a bowl of icing.

My Naughty Little Puppy

Ellie covered her cakes in primrose
yellow icing with sugar flowers on top.

"They're brilliant," Lucy said admiringly.
"Oh, look!"

A little brown and white face was
peering sadly in at the kitchen window.

"Rascal!" Ellie gasped. "He must have
climbed on to the bench."

My Naughty Little Puppy

"I'll pop out and have a game of fetch
with him," Dad said, smiling.

Ellie watched through the window as
Dad gently lifted Rascal down. She
was having a lovely time, of course
she was, but she wished Rascal
could be there with her. She could
hear Dad calling to Rascal as she
put her cakes on the stand.
Everyone's cakes were different.
Christy and Jessie had gone mad
with sprinkles, and Lucy's had
delicate spirals of silver balls.

"Ugh, Max...!" Lila sighed, and
everyone looked over at his cake.

"I didn't even know we had black
food colouring." Mum shook her head.

My Naughty Little Puppy

 "That's going at the back of the cake stand," Ellie told him, glaring at his black cake, decorated with a purple spider's web.

"Leave them all to set, girls. Why don't you go and try the dance game?" Mum suggested.

"Great!" Max groaned. He headed upstairs, and Ellie and her friends raced into the living room to set up the PlayStation with Lucy's dance game.

"I'm a terrible dancer," Jessie giggled, as Lucy tried out some warm-up moves.

"I bet you're not, and anyway it doesn't matter," Lucy promised. "It's just fun. You get to do all these cool moves. Come on, it's starting!

Chapter Ten

Things That Go Bump in the Night

"Oh, I can't move after all the pizza and cake I ate!" Ellie flumped on to the sofa.

"Shall we change into our pyjamas and get our sleeping bags out?" Christy suggested. "I stashed a big bar of chocolate in my bag for the midnight feast," she added in a whisper.

Ellie bounced up again, tiredness suddenly forgotten. "Oh, yes." *I can say a quick hello to Rascal too,* she told herself.

My Naughty Little Puppy

He was probably feeling very confused, being shunted in and out of the garden to stay out of Lucy's way. She popped into the kitchen to see him on the way back from fetching her sleeping bag and pyjamas, and Rascal licked her lovingly.

"Come on, Ellie!" Lydia called, and Ellie ran to join everyone spreading out their sleeping bags in a row on the floor. They snuggled up in them, gossiping about school. Christy was just explaining that she hoped they didn't get Miss Casey next year, when Ellie realized Lucy had gone silent. She peered over at her. Only Lucy's nose was sticking out of her sleeping bag. "Are you OK?" she whispered, nudging Lucy and trying not to be too obvious.

My Naughty Little Puppy

"Mm," murmured Lucy.

"You don't sound very OK."

"I miss my mum," Lucy sniffed. "I haven't been to a sleepover before."

"I haven't either. Do you want to go home?" Ellie asked, hoping Lucy would say no.

"Please don't!" Christy butted in.

Lucy smiled tearily at her. "I don't really

want to, it's just..." She rubbed her eyes on
the edge of her sleeping bag. "I can't cheer
myself up. And I forgot to bring my bear..."

Ellie chewed her lip. It was a pity that
Lucy didn't like dogs. Rascal could cheer
anybody up. There was silence for a
moment, the only noise was Lucy obviously
trying not to cry. Ellie put an arm round her,
wondering what to do.

My Naughty Little Puppy

"Eeek!" Lucy suddenly squeaked, and
Ellie yelped too.

"What is it? Oh! Sorry, Lucy, I'll take him
out. I can't have shut the kitchen door
properly."

Rascal was standing on the end of
Lucy's sleeping bag, his tail wagging
madly. Dangling from his mouth was Ellie's
missing pink birthday rabbit.

My Naughty Little Puppy

"He brought me a rabbit!" Lucy was staring at Rascal in amazement. "Because I forgot my bear!"

Ellie opened her mouth – and then shut it again and nodded solemnly. She thought it was probably a complete accident, but if it cheered Lucy up, it didn't matter.

Rascal nudged the rabbit towards Lucy, and then sat down proudly on her feet, with his head hopefully on one side.

"Good dog..." Lucy whispered. Then she actually took one hand out of her sleeping bag, and slowly patted Rascal on the head.

My Naughty Little Puppy

"Time to go to sleep now, girls! Night!"
Mum called.

Everyone was silent as they heard Ellie's
mum and dad going up the stairs. Then
Christy flicked her torch back on, and they
went on chatting. Rascal was curled up
asleep on top of Ellie now. Lucy had said
she didn't mind if he stayed. His loan of the
pink rabbit seemed to have won her over
completely.

"Can you hear a funny noise?" Jessie
asked, a little while later. Lucy and Lydia
were dozing, and Jessie and Ellie and
Christy had just been whispering quietly to
each other, nearly asleep themselves.

"Sounds like someone coming down the
stairs," Ellie murmured. "Christy, turn off your

torch, Mum thinks we're asleep!"

The door creaked open, but instead of Ellie's mum come to check on them, an eerie white shape floated in the doorway.

Lydia woke up and screamed as the shape let out a long, spooky moan.

"A ghost!" Jessie gasped, pulling her sleeping bag over her head.

My Naughty Little Puppy

Ellie's heart was thudding horribly, but there was something familiar about that moaning. Rascal was growling on her lap, and suddenly he let out an ear-splitting bark, and dashed at the ghostly figure, leaping up at it.

"Rascal, come back!" Ellie wailed, not wanting him to be hurt by whatever it was.

But the ghost let out a loud and unghostly yelp as Rascal jumped up again, and then it fell over backwards. Rascal ran happily back to Ellie, dragging the corner of a white bed sheet in his teeth.

"Max!" Ellie hissed, climbing out of her sleeping bag and snapping on the light. "I can't believe you'd do that! Mum'll kill you!"

My Naughty Little Puppy

Ellie grabbed her pillow and whacked Max over the head with it, and Christy and the others joined in, giggling as he squealed for mercy.

"That's not fair! I'm outnumbered! Oof!" he yelped, as Lydia got him in the stomach with her pillow.

Rascal jumped on to Max's feet and

My Naughty Little Puppy

joined in, barking happily, and tearing at Ellie's pillow with his teeth. A cloud of feathers filled the room, and Rascal sneezed in surprise.

"Hang on, don't let him get up!" Ellie grabbed her birthday camera, and snapped Max, wailing with laughter and covered in feathers.

My Naughty Little Puppy

There was a sound of running footsteps on the stairs, and Mum appeared, looking annoyed.

"What's going on?" she demanded.

"They attacked me!" Max staggered to his feet.

"And what were you doing down here in the first place?" Mum snapped. "It's nearly midnight, and just look at all this mess!" She sighed. "We'll have to clear it up tomorrow. Now go to sleep, all of you!"

The girls giggled as Max trailed out of the door after Mum.

My Naughty Little Puppy

"Lucy! Your mum's here!" Ellie's mum put
her head round the living-room door,
where the girls were sleepily watching a
DVD. It was ten in the morning, but
everyone was still feeling happily tired.
Ellie's mum had let them eat the muffins
she'd got for breakfast on the sofa.
Everyone had been hungry – they'd all
been too tired to have their midnight feast
after the pillow fight.

"Hi, Mum!"

Lucy's mother stared back at her in
amazement. Rascal was lying half on Ellie
and half on Lucy, snoozing. Here and there
a little white feather was dotted in his fur,

and a rather battered-looking pink rabbit was between his paws.

"But – you're scared of dogs..." Lucy's mum sounded as though she couldn't believe what she was seeing.

"Not Rascal." Lucy patted him. "He's lovely."

Ellie smiled proudly. Nobody could resist her Rascal!

"Thanks for inviting me to your party, Ellie." Lucy hugged her, then gave Rascal a final goodbye stroke. "It was the best sleepover ever!"

Ellie beamed, and Rascal lifted his head and yawned hugely. Sleepovers were brilliant fun – Ellie and Rascal both agreed – but they were definitely tiring!

WOOF

magazine

Out now

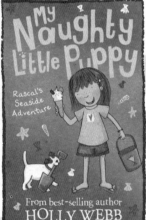

It's the summer holidays, and Ellie and her family are off to stay at their grandparents' house by the sea! Ellie can't wait to take Rascal on his first holiday, but will he behave, or get sent home in disgrace?

Happy Pupday!

How about celebrating your pup's birthday with a doggy party? If you don't know when he was born, you can celebrate the day you got him – it's a happy anniversary for both of you!

🐾 Invite: your friends and their dogs round to your garden or a local park that allows dogs.

🐾 Theme: "famous dogs", such as the 101 Dalmatians, Scooby Doo, Gromit, Lassie, and Lady and the Tramp. Ask your guests to dress up as famous dog owners, e.g. in *The Wizard of Oz*, Toto's owner Dorothy wore a checked dress with red sparkly shoes!

🐾 Cake: there are many special dog cake recipes online, so ask an adult to help you bake one. But remember to get one that your friends can eat, too!

🐾 Party games: People vs Pooch races, Frisbee, and a treasure hunt with dog treats as prizes.

🐾 Don't forget a present for your pup. What about a T-shirt for your dog or a new collar?